Published by Familius™ LLC, www.familius.com
1254 Commerce Way Sanger, CA 93657

Familius books are available at special discounts for bulk purchases, whether
for sales promotions or for family or corporate use. For more information,
contact Familius Sales at 559-876-2170 or email orders@familius.com.

Library of Congress Control Number 2020938231
ISBN 9781641702898 eISBN 9781641703833
KF 9781641704076   FE 9781641704311

Printed in China
Edited by Christopher Robbins & Brooke Jorden
Book design by Brent Watts
Cover design by Carlos Guerrero

10 9 8 7 6 5 4 3 2 1

BY RUSSELL HICKS & MATT CUBBERLY
ILLUSTRATIONS BY RYLEY GARCIA

Everyone knows the story of Santa Claus, delivering gifts to millions of children in one night. It was a big job, but Santa and his North Pole team di it every year.

But times change, and eventually, Santa made a BIG mistake. He knew it was time to modernize, so he created....

"And that's where we are today, my boy," says Grandpa Elf, closing a dusty old book. Yo-Yo, a pint-sized elf, loves Grandpa's stories of Christmases past.

"Now hurry along," Grandpa says. "You wouldn't want to be late for your first day at the workshop!"

Yo-Yo looks around the factory full of robotic candy cane arms and flying peppermint drones. *Where's the Christmas magic like in Grandpa's book?* Yo-Yo wonders. *The reindeer? The sleigh? Santa?!*

The cheery voice of Cookie, the HR elf,
booms out over the factory's loudspeaker:

"Remember, Christmas cannot make itself.
We need the work of every elf!"

Yo-Yo sighs and presses a button again. A robotic
arm loads a drone with a brightly wrapped gift.

Suddenly, a shrieking alarm pierces through the factory!
Red warning lights flash and the conveyor belts grind to a halt!

"All elves to the Wrapping Room to hear about the impending doom!"

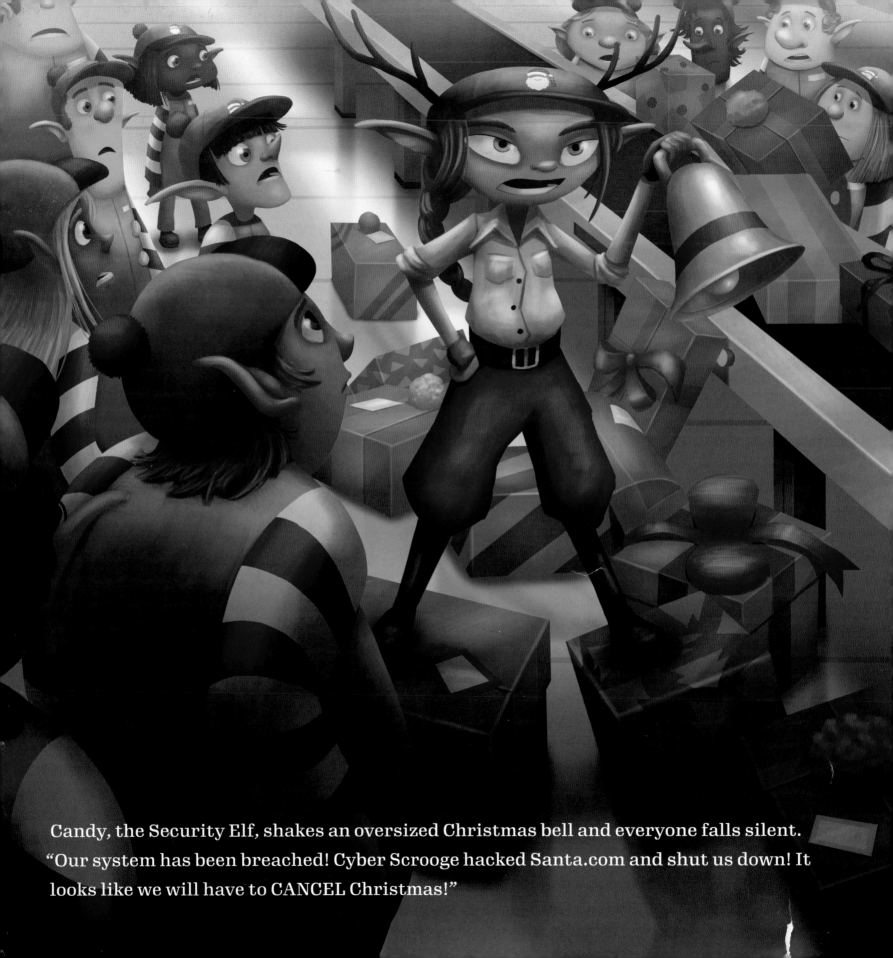

Candy, the Security Elf, shakes an oversized Christmas bell and everyone falls silent. "Our system has been breached! Cyber Scrooge hacked Santa.com and shut us down! It looks like we will have to CANCEL Christmas!"

The elves panic as Yo-Yo slowly raises his hand.
"I have an idea . . ."

"We can save Christmas! We just need to find the sleigh and the reindeer . . . and Santa!"

Cookie thinks over Yo-Yo's plan for a moment. "Christmas needs us. It's all gone wrong. So I can help and come along!"

Candy stands as well. "Count me in too!"

Yo-Yo, Cookie, and Candy take flight to cheers from down below. Candy asks, "Well, Yo-Yo, where to first?"

"First, we need the sleigh. Grandpa's book says, *The Big Apple* . . . do you think Santa's sleigh is in New York City?"

"Anything can happen in a New York minute," Cookie says. "Let's hit the city and go find it."

"This isn't right!" Yo-Yo says as he looks at the sad, broken-down sleigh.
"How can we save Christmas without Santa's sleigh?"

"Santa's sleigh?' a man says. "*The* sleigh?" Yo-Yo and Cookie nod.

"Don't you worry, little elves. I can fix it! Santa's sleigh will be flying again before you can say 'fruitcake stomachache'!"

"And I'll stay to help," Candy says. "You can count on us!"

"Now off to find the reindeer! Grandpa's book says they retired to Taymyr—Russia!"

"Oh no!" says Yo-Yo, looking at the lazy reindeer.

"These reindeer can't pull anything, let alone fly."

But Cookie spots a group of children nearby. "These reindeer are not fit to fly, nor help deliver each child's toy. To get them back in shape and spry, we need the help of each girl and boy!"

Yo-Yo looks again at Grandpa's book and reads, *A well-deserved rest—the Caribbean!*
Yo-Yo spots Santa's RV on a quiet beach and lands. But where is Santa?

Suddenly, a faint

HO HO HO

rings out over the waves. Yo-Yo looks to the sky and sees a small red dot.

It gets bigger and LOUDER!

HO HO HO

Santa glides down and Yo-Yo explains everything.

"I see," Santa says. "And I know just where we must go next."

They land before a small,
undecorated house—
not a wreath or
twinkling light in sight.

"That, my little Yo-Yo, is the headquarters
of Cyber Scrooge," Santa whispers.

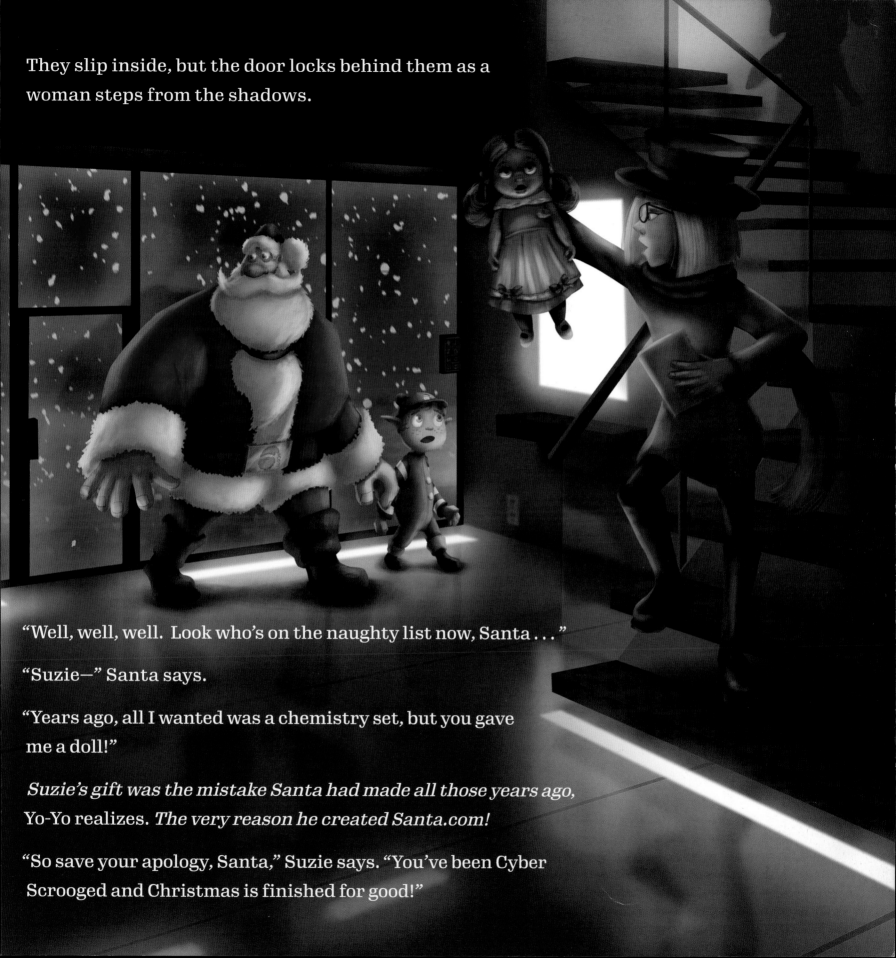

They slip inside, but the door locks behind them as a woman steps from the shadows.

"Well, well, well. Look who's on the naughty list now, Santa . . ."

"Suzie—" Santa says.

"Years ago, all I wanted was a chemistry set, but you gave me a doll!"

Suzie's gift was the mistake Santa had made all those years ago, Yo-Yo realizes. *The very reason he created Santa.com!*

"So save your apology, Santa," Suzie says. "You've been Cyber Scrooged and Christmas is finished for good!"

Just then, a small girl appears. "Who are you?" she asks Santa.

"Hello there, Ella. My name is Santa Claus."

"Santa?! My mom said you weren't coming this year!"

"Not coming? You've been a very good girl, and I've brought you something special."

"A soccer ball! It's just what I wanted! How did you know?"

ELLA

"Well, Ella, years ago, I made a BIG mistake, and another little girl didn't get what she wished for. From now on I'll make my list and check it THRICE to make sure that never happens again."

Ella runs to her mother to show her the gift. Suzie quickly wipes away a tear.

Suzie gives Santa a warm hug. "I'm so sorry, Santa. I thought you just didn't care."

Santa shakes his head. "No, no, no. The mistake was all mine."

"But I've made such a mess of things," Susie says. "How can we ever save Christmas?"

Yo-Yo quickly raises his hand. "I have an idea!"

"You saved Christmas, Yo-Yo," Santa says. "And more importantly, you reminded us that Christmas isn't about deadlines or shiny production lines. It's about the Christmas spirit and giving with love."

Yo-Yo smiles and closes Grandpa Elf's book. "And so, my little elves, that's the story of my first day at Santa.com. Now, off you all go. You wouldn't want to be late for YOUR first day!"